THREESOMES EROTICA

AND MARIA
MAKES THREE

Joan Vegas

WARNING

This book contains sexually explicit scenes and adult language. It may be considered offensive to some readers. This book is for sale to adults ONLY.

* * * * * * * * * * * * * * * * * * *

Please store your files wisely where they cannot be accessed by underage readers.

Please feel free to send me an email. Just know that these emails are filtered by my publisher. Good news is always welcome.

Joan Vegas - **joan_vegas@awesomeauthors.org**

You might also want to check my blog for Updates and interesting info.
http://joan-vegas.awesomeauthors.org/

About the Publisher

4Fun Publishing, a member of **BLVNP Incorporated**, 340 S. Lemon #6200, Walnut CA 91789, info@blvnp.com / legal@blvnp.com
NOTE: Due to the highly emotional reaction of some people to works of erotic fiction, any email sent to the above address that contains foul language or religious references is automatically deleted by our anti-spam software and will not be seen. All other communications are welcome.

DISCLAIMER

Please don't be stupid and kill yourself. This book is a work of FICTION. Do not try any new sexual practice that you find in this book. It is fiction and not to be confused with reality. Neither the author nor the publisher or its associates assume any responsibility for any loss, injury, death or legal consequences resulting from acting on the contents in this book. Every character in this book is over 18 years of age. The author's opinions are not to be construed as the opinions of the publisher. The material in this book is for entertainment purposes ONLY. Enjoy.

And Maria Makes Three

Threesomes Erotica

By: Joan Vegas

ISBN: 978-1-68030-138-0

Letters to Joan

This is another in a series of tantalizing reports received by Joan Vegas from her readers… about especially memorable erotic experiences, written by the people who enjoyed them. In this case a loving couple invites a younger woman to become part of their shared sex life. That led to her moving in to create a long-term FMF three-way relationship.

Joan believes all women need more than one sexual playmate if they are going to experience their feminine pleasure potential. She has created her own long-term partnership with two loving guys, and together they have built a family and explored alternative playmates. She has published reports on their special family and their sexually-fulfilling experiences. As a result she receives reports from many of her readers. That is where this report originated. Joan's role is to do minor editing and change names.

And Maria Makes Three

Dear Ms. Joan:

This is the report you asked me to write up about me, my husband and our very dear friend (and special family member), Maria.

Let me begin by telling you about each of us.

About me (Annette)… Since the first time I had intercourse in the backseat of a boyfriend's car, I have always enjoyed the feelings of pleasure that sex has given me. While I had feelings of conflict over the non-marital sex those first few times, I still enjoyed the feel of a man's organ probing around inside me. Then I learned to give my dates manual and oral pleasure. I found that I liked that too.

A few years later one of the guys I dated treated me to "head." I was hesitant at first to let him do that, but he insisted. The intense pleasure of that experience left me wanting "head" as often as a date would give it to me.

That was my sexual background prior to meeting Jordan (or Jordy, as I call him). From our earliest dates, we made sex a regular part of our dates. Six months after we met, we married. At the time, Jordy was 24 and I was 23.

Oh yes, the obligatory physical description. I stand 5' 6" tall, generally weigh about 130 lbs., and have rather full C-cup boobs. My eyes are blue, and my hair is a sort of dishwater blond. I generally keep my hair curled and styled.

While I have always thought of myself as sort of average, Jordy is constantly telling me that I am "really good lookin' with beautiful legs and tits." Who am I to disagree with him?

Both Jordy and I are college grads with post-grad degrees. For the past several years I have been doing contract engineering work out of our home. My field of engineering allows me to get work rather easily, and choose between part time or full time work.

About Jordy... Jordy is very handsome (in my subjective opinion, but Maria says so too). He stands 5' 9" tall, typically weighs about 170 lbs., and has brown hair and brown eyes. He has a ruddy complexion, a mustache and a full beard. Jordy sports a cock that when stimulated measures 8" long and 5" around.

Unlike most other men I have seen, his dick tapers from a relatively small head to its thick girth (gives wonderful sensations as it enters and slides within my pussy!).

Both Jordy and I generally work full time. He works for a computer firm that sells and services software for specialty retailing businesses. His work often takes him out on the road (up to 1,000 miles away). We are both typical Anglo-Saxon Caucasians.

About Maria... Maria is a beautiful young woman (four years younger than me). Her father was half black and half American Indian. Her mother was mostly Spanish (her mother from Mexico and father from Brazil).

The result of their union was a sexy gal who has soft skin that boasts the appearance of a year-round deep Coppertone tan. Jordy says her skin looks (and tastes like) golden honey.

She has small cone-shaped breasts with large (very sensitive) nipples. Her legs are at least as long as mine, yet she just stands just 5'3" tall. Jordy describes her as "a compact gal whose legs go all the way to 'heaven'". The little nymph typically weighs in at a scant 105 lbs.

Maria was born in Porto Rico, and grew up in New Jersey. Her father died when she was very young. Her mother struggled to raise her and her two older sisters. When they grew up, the sisters left home, and really have not made much of themselves. Maria saw that, and determined that she was going to get some higher education and make something of herself.

They both also had very unsatisfying marriages to husbands who were abusive. Maria's mother got sick when Maria was just 17, and Maria decided to stay living at home and help her mother.

Meanwhile, Maria enrolled at a local community college while staying at home to care for her mother.

Her mother died just after Maria turned 20. With nothing holding her back any more, and no desire to hook up with some guy just to get married, Maria decided to travel west to begin a new life. Her savings took her only to Oklahoma City where she got work in a restaurant. After several months, she decided she didn't like Oklahoma City. She had accumulated enough money for a bus ticket to Santa Fe, New Mexico, where we happened to be living at the time.

Again, Maria took work waiting tables in a restaurant. That's where we met her, three weeks after her arrival. While dining at the restaurant where she was working, we got to talking with her. We found her to be quite attractive, pleasantly personable, and quite intelligent. She agreed to meet us for a drink after her shift ended.

We walked down the street to a nearby lounge where we each had a few drinks and got to know each other. We learned that Maria had her 21st birthday the week before, so we asked her if she would like to celebrate by joining us for a late night dip at a nearby hot springs. She said she did not have her swimsuit with her. I let her know that the place has several pools, some of which were "clothing optional," and that we seldom wore swim suits there. After giggling a bit about that prospect, she agreed, and we all piled into our car for the short trip.

I should tell you that Maria has long, straight, shiny black hair that hangs about 5" below her shoulders. Her eyes are also pools of deep black. In spite of her father's racial background, Maria's face and hair give no indication of her Black heritage. Only her skin evidences her mixed heritage... and does so in a highly attractive way.

As she and I stripped in the dressing room, I noticed she had a full, untrimmed bush covering her crotch. We both used our towels to cover ourselves on the short walk to the pool that Jordy had picked out. We slipped in on either side of him, and began to chat like we had been long-time friends. During our time in the pool, a few others joined us for a while. When I sat on the edge of the pool to cool off, Maria joined me with no evidence of concern about her nudity in the dim light.

During our conversations we let Maria know that we had a sort of open marriage, and had each occasionally enjoyed having others as sex partners. She just took it all in without any particular reaction.

Getting to Know Maria... At the end of the evening we took Maria to her apartment and made arrangements for the three of us to go out together again the following Saturday night. That night Jordy and I made passionate love as I told him that no other woman had ever turned me on before... but that Maria had. He suggested that just maybe, Maria might be a woman we could both enjoy... while giving her pleasure.

Saturday night involved drinks again, dancing, and then another trip to the hot springs. While at the springs, I suggested that Maria spend the night with us. She was thoroughly enjoying our growing friendship, and she readily agreed.

At home Maria and I decided to take a brief shower to get the minerals off our bodies. She mentioned that she did not have any sleepwear with her. I laughed and said, "No problem. We always sleep nude, and we have all seen each other nude anyway."

When we got out of the shower she and I wrapped towels around our waists and ended up on our living room floor, watching TV while Jordy took a shower. While Jordy was gone, Maria mentioned that she had noticed how neat and well-trimmed my pussy looked, particularly compared to her untrimmed dark bush. I told her I was sure we could take care of that... if she wanted. When Jordy returned, he hadn't even bothered wrapping a towel around himself.

I told Jordy about Maria's comments, and he asked her if she would like a custom trim job. I pointed out that it was Jordy who always kept my bush well-trimmed. Maria was a bit hesitant at first, but I grabbed the blanket off the couch, encouraged her to lie back onto it, and said, "Let's get that pussy of yours looking sharp." Jordy rounded up the scissors, shaving gear and clippers... and returned.

Jordy went to work cropping her pussy hair shorter, and then shaved each side so she ended up with a V-shaped arrow of cropped hair aiming directly at her clit. Meanwhile, Maria and I talked girl-talk, and every once in a while she let out a giggle and said, "That tickles." When Jordy was done, I got a mirror and let her inspect her new look.

That's when Jordy said, "Lay back. There is one more thing I have to do." She did.

He had been crouched between her legs as he worked on her. He took the warm wash cloth we had been using to wipe away the trimmed hair, and gave her pussy one more swash before bending over her crotch and placing the tip of his tongue on her newly-exposed clit. I heard Maria let out a little gasp, and saw her eyes close... but she didn't move away from Jordy's ministrations.

As Jordy began to lick and suck Maria's pussy, he reached up, took one of my hands, and placed it on one of Maria's breasts. With my hand under his, he began to caress her breast. Then he took his hand away and moved it to Maria's other breast, leaving me to caress her on my own. Soon we were both manipulating her small cone-shaped breasts and nipples.

Clearly Maria was not offended. With her eyes still closed, she was giving signs of full, relaxed enjoyment of the scene.

A few times Maria's body shook, evidencing mini-orgasms. Finally Jordy rose up, looked at me and whispered, "Your turn." As he backed out from between Maria's legs, I grasped what he meant. He was suggesting that I take his place and begin tonguing Maria's pussy and clit. Then I remembered having told him that Maria turned me on.

I thought, 'What the heck', and moved between her legs as Jordy moved up on Maria's opposite side. He began kissing and sucking her nipples as I lowered my head for the first time to the pussy of another woman. Maria was a bit taken aback when she realized that Jordy and I had switched places. Jordy just said, "Shhh" and she relaxed to the feel of a woman's tongue on her clit and pussy. It was a first for her too.

As I began to get into the special taste of Maria's pussy, and the passion of the moment, I began letting my tongue probe deeply into our new friend's freshly shaven cunt. I guess I really got into it. Soon Maria was writhing on the floor below me, and then she let out a loud "Ah..." as she squirmed and pressed her crotch up against my face. She was obviously enjoying another orgasm... an even larger one that time.

Well, to make a long story shorter, we all ended up on the king-size bed that Jordy and I share. First I was in the middle, and Jordy took me missionary style as Maria and I cuddled and kissed. Jordy brought me to a wonderful climax just as he shot his load into me. After a rest, with them on either side of me... hands exploring each other's bodies... we got Jordy on his back between us, facing up. Maria and I took turns with our hands stroking his cock to stiffness again.

Then I mounted Jordy's face, facing down across his body, and got Maria to mount his cock. She didn't hesitate. As we rode him, we were both giggling... and soon playing with each other's breasts. Jordy sucked me to another enjoyable orgasm as Maria increased her tempo pumping herself up and down on his cock. She shuddered in another climax as Jordy just kept pressing his groin up into her. Clearly, he was still hot for more.

I moved from Jordy's face to straddle his cock, letting Maria cuddle in next to Jordy. He and I kept up a vigorous fucking action as he kissed Maria's forehead, neck and lips (while fondling her breasts). I had another orgasm and flopped over onto Jordy's other side. He still had not come a second time.

After a period of three-way hugging, kissing and mutual fondling, Jordy convinced Maria to assume the doggy position near the end of the bed.

He got up, stood behind her, and slowly inserted himself deeply into her again. As he started a slow fucking action, she looked over at me and mouthed the words "Is this really OK with you?" I responded by reaching over, hugging her against my breasts and whispering, "Absolutely. Enjoy yourself!"

Well, they fucked like that for some time before they both exploded in evening-ending orgasms... while I played with Maria's silky hair and breasts. We all soon fell asleep.

The next morning (a Sunday) we all slept in. When Maria and I did finally wake up, Jordy already had the coffee on and was frying some eggs. I loaned Maria a robe. Jordy had just his under shorts on. We just ate like that, and talked about the fun we had all shared the night before.

A Little More Background about Jordy and Me... As mentioned above, I was not a novice to sex before meeting Jordy, but my experiences had been fairly conventional. That was true for Jordy too... mainly fairly conventional date sex, and always heterosexual.

Sometime after we were married, we got to talking one night and ended up agreeing on two basic tenants of human sexuality. First, we agreed in principle that everyone (men and women both) occasionally need to experience the variety of different sex partners in their life.

We had talked with enough of our married friends to know that many of them had side affairs (both the men and the women), and several of those affairs had resulted in marriage breakups or severely damaged relationships. We did not ever want our relationship to break up or be damaged, so we agreed that secret affairs were not for us, and yet we would recognize each other's need for periodic variety.

Second, we both acknowledged that the biological make-up of the male makes him less able to enjoy prolonged sexual pleasure than the female, and that the result was that the female (in our case... me) seldom experienced sexual fulfillment at a level that she could.

Fortunately for me, Jordy loves to go down on me for an extended period before he tries to enter me. However, like most guys we know of, Jordy usually climaxes pretty fast once he gets his cock inside my pussy and starts to pump. With some rest, Jordy can restore his erection and then go for a second, longer round of screwing. It's that second round that generally gives me the most pleasure.

However, that first round generally gets my juices flowing, and I feel rather let down having to wait for him to recover for round two. And, even after round two, I often feel like the intensity of my multiple orgasms is still far short of where it could be. Often, after resting (which causes my libido to diminish), we do continue in shared sex play. But I always felt that if I had another lover to keep me going, my fulfillment could be even more satisfying.

We had heard about "swinging," and decided to check it out. It was a mutual decision... neither pushing the other toward the idea. After some research, we learned that there were a couple of different swinging groups in our area. We made contact with one of them, and were invited to an "on-premise swing party" that the group regularly hosted. We decided to check it out on a no-commitment basis.

The party was held in a private home out in the country. The home was well separated from other houses, and had an outdoor swimming pool, surrounded by high walls. When we got there we discovered more than a dozen couples, of varying ages and body descriptions, cavorting around the pool in the nude. Having no problem with nudity (we have both done our share of skinny-dipping over the years), we shed our clothes and joined them.

We found that several of the couples were quite nice and hospitable. Eventually we noticed that folks were pairing off (usually not with their spouse) and heading to other rooms of the house. One of those rooms had been designated "the orgy room". It was large enough to accommodate several people at once, and had wall-to-wall mattresses. That first night, Jordy and I kept together, and we decided to spend some time in that room and watch what others were doing.

No surprise. The folks in there were doing just about everything. We found a corner, sat on the mattress-covered floor with our backs against the wall and watched. The action soon got us hot, and we began playing with each other. One guy came up and asked if he could join us. I just replied, "Not yet". Jordy ended up screwing me as we watched sex play by the others in twos, threes and more. We both had wonderful orgasms. Then we left.

Our First Experiences with New Sex Partners... A couple weeks later we went back again. That time when a guy asked me to join him in the orgy room, Jordy said, "Go ahead hon!" I did. In the room, the guy kissed me while we were still standing, running his hands all over my body. It felt so good that I was trembling. He suggested that I lay down on the soft floor. I did, and he began to lick my legs and thighs, working his way to my pussy.

About that time, I noticed Jordy walk into the dimly lit room with a lady. They ended up just a few feet away from me, so I was able to watch as Jordy ate, and then screwed the unknown woman. When he finished up, he caught my eye and winked at me. My playmate was just starting to screw me. I winked back at Jordy, and then let my body give itself up to the sensations of having a new cock buried inside me. I truly enjoyed that screw!

A little while later Jordy and I met up at the pool where we exchanged details about our first "other person" experiences. It had proven to be a good evening with genuine pleasure for both of us. When we got home we screwed some more and giggled a bit as we told each other about our evening's "lovers".

Since then, before meeting Maria, we occasionally (every 6 to 8 weeks) returned to the swing parties. We never really got heavy into the swinging scene, but the experiences we had were fun. And, we met some really friendly people. One of the couples we met turned us on to a couple of single guys who they occasionally met with "for her pleasure." Single guys were not allowed at the regular swing parties, but we learned that several of those at the parties occasionally had single guys or gals join them at their homes.

Jordy contacted one of the single guys and surprised me one evening by inviting him to our place. That was one stellar evening! After I showered, they both joined in giving me an oral bath like I had never experienced before. Then Jordy asked the other guy to "screw her real good". It was a good screw too. As quickly as the guy was done, Jordy entered me and gave me another good screw. By the time Jordy was done, the other guy had recovered, and as Jordy pulled out, he pressed his cock back into me.

He screwed me through three more delightful orgasms before shooting another load into me. Jordy entered me again right after our guest pulled out, and we had one last, leisurely screw before bidding our guest farewell. That was the only time we had a threesome before we met Maria.

That night proved to me that my earlier feelings had been correct. Having a second lover... along with Jordy... clearly did allow me to have longer, uninterrupted stimulation... enabling me to enjoy sexual pleasure at a much more intense level than I had ever experienced before. I loved it!

Building Our Relationship with Maria... After that first overnight session with Maria, we began having her spend weekends with us on a regular basis. ALL of us always enjoyed every form of intimacy that we explored together... and we let ourselves explore everything! Both Maria and I broke down all of our barriers regarding girl-girl intimacy. Neither of us considered ourselves gay... and the "bi" label never came up.

With the three of us regularly playing together in bed, both Maria and I got to regularly experience the extended, uninterrupted sexual stimulation that I first experienced when Jordy brought that extra guy home to give me doubled pleasure that first time. Jordy would go down on both of us as we cuddled and caressed each other's bodies. Then he would take turns screwing us.

We quickly got to a point where the one who had just benefited from Jordy's cock action would be kept at a peak of pleasure by the other one, until Jordy was ready to go again. Sometimes we would soothe each other's overheated (just fucked) pussy with our tongue, and savor Jordy's deposits while waiting for his return to action.

Sometimes we would 69 each other and let Jordy press that wonderful cock of his into the topside pussy as we sucked the adjacent clit. Other times we would form a triangle on the bed with Jordy's cock buried in one of our pussies as he ate the other one, and as we cuddled, kissed and played with each other's breasts.

When Jordy was not around, Maria and I enjoyed lots of girl-talk. During one of those sessions she admitted that she was getting frustrated with her lot in life. She was observing the way both Jordy and I enjoy our work, yet she felt she was going nowhere. She admitted that she had always wanted to be a nurse, but had never been able to save enough money to start nursing school. Her job gave her minimal income, and her regular living expenses consumed most of what she made. We started brainstorming.

We figured that if she could minimize her living expenses, and get a better job, she could save for school. Then, if she got a decent part-time job, she could work enough to meet her needs while going to school.

We both agreed to think about her dilemma, to see if we could think of ways to get her into school and on her way to the nursing career she had always wanted.

A few nights later I mentioned the situation to Jordy. I pointed out our extra bedroom in our basement, and suggested that maybe we could help Maria cut her living expenses by letting her live with us. We also have our offices in the basement. The basement bedroom was seldom used, except for occasional mid-day romps when the two of us were so inclined. Meanwhile, Jordy talked to some of his friends and ended up getting Maria a good-paying receptionist job at a local real estate company. Finally, Jordy and I agreed to let Maria move in with us so she could save most of her new earnings.

I met with Maria for lunch during her first week in her new receptionist position. She loved her new job. Then I told her what Jordy and I had decided. I let her know that she could help me cook and clean house as pay for her room and board, would not need her own phone (unless she wanted one), and could use our extra car (an old one we had not been using) to get back and forth to work (and eventually to school).

I let her know that I had just one important concern. I knew she was on birth control pills all the time while we had been playing, but I wanted her to know that if she ever got pregnant by Jordy, it would irreparably damage our special three-way relationship.

I also told her that I was thinking that sometime in the future I planned to get off my birth control so Jordy and I could have a baby. I told her that when I did drop my birth control, until I was sure I was pregnant by Jordy, I would not be letting any other guy screw me.

Maria assured me that she agreed with my conclusion that she must never allow a situation to exist where her fun with Jordy might result in her pregnancy. Yet, she told me that someday she, too, might like to have a baby. She said that having watched her sister's lives, she had no desire to marry, but that when her situation was right, she would like to have a child that she could raise on her own. Once again, she assured me that if she ever did decide to get pregnant she would tell me in advance, and together we would plan for her pregnancy by someone other than Jordy.

Maria Moved In... Shortly after our conversation, Maria moved in with us. She and I worked together to fix up the spare bedroom as her new home. She began taking on most of my housework and prepared many of our meals.

Naturally, our three-way sex play continued... and grew. Maria regularly spent 2 or 3 nights a week in our bed at night. Sometimes when I wasn't in the mood for sex, I sent Jordy down to her room to spend the night with her. Other times when Jordy was on a business trip, Maria would sleep with me and we enjoyed lots of girl-girl intimacy and cuddling.

From the time we met Maria, she would occasionally date guys. With our encouragement, that continued after she moved into our home and became an equal partner in "our family". Our basement has garden-level access from the back, so she was able to come and go with a degree of privacy. Sometimes she brought home male guests to spend the night with her. Neither Jordy nor I had any problems with Maria's private life.

We met many of the men Maria dated. For the most part, they didn't know of the intimate three-way relationship we shared. However, when a couple of Maria's dates proved to be open-minded, and got along well with Jordy... we ended up inviting them (individually) to join us for some four-way fun. I got to enjoy some new "stuff," and Jordy always enjoyed bedding Maria. Sometimes all three of them would join in pleasuring me... or the two guys and I would make Maria the center of our erotic attentions.

We occasionally took Maria with us to swing club parties. She was well received, and always enjoyed herself. A few of the couples from those parties invited Maria to join them in three-way fun. She seemed to enjoy the periodic variety. And, Jordy continued to occasionally bring a new guy home to join him in doubling my pleasure... and Maria's too.

Maria finally saved up enough to enroll in nursing school. She cut her hours back at the real estate office (they liked her so much that they were willing to accommodate her schedule), and she entered school. Maria had completed two years of community college back in New Jersey. Maria's time at her nursing school extended over almost two years.

Having earned her nursing license, Maria began working in a local hospital. Soon she was able to purchase her own car. Yet, she still enjoyed living with us... and we thoroughly enjoyed having her part of our special family.

That's about the time I decided it was now or never... if I was going to have a baby. I talked it over with both Jordy and Maria, and took myself off birth control. Jordy was enjoying our "let's make a baby" sex each day. I had only been off birth control a few weeks when Maria came to me and said, "Wouldn't it be neat if we both had a baby about the same time? They could grow up together."

I hesitated at first, reminding her that Jordy could NOT be the father of her child. She again reaffirmed her agreement with me, but added that she was sure she could find a sperm donor for herself. Over the next few days we talked the subject over with Jordy. He agreed that it might be nice to have two young ones growing up together in our household, but pointed out one potential problem.

"What if Maria's 'sperm donor' wants to play a role in her new child's life?" Maria and I talked about that risk, if she got pregnant by a guy who could ultimately find out that he was the father. Maria was a bit dejected for a few days. Then Jordy came up with an idea.

He suggested planning a special gang-bang party for Maria... out of town... after she was off birth control pills and was at a peak fertility period. He pointed out that we could control who was invited, we could use fictitious names, and the guys would never learn that their sperm had been used to impregnate Maria. The more he developed his idea and shared it with us, the more Maria liked it. She decided to go for it.

Maria immediately stopped taking her birth control pills. Jordy immediately stopped having intercourse with her (but we all had lots of other continuing sex play), and she began monitoring her menstrual cycle. Maria also stopped seeing other guys during that period.

A Gang-Bang for Maria...

Jordy decided that Las Vegas would be the ideal setting for our planned "Gang-bang for Maria." About that time I discovered that I was clearly pregnant. The "let's make a baby" play that Jordy and I had been engaging in (often with Maria at our side) had worked.

As I began to relish my new pregnancy, Jordy began responding to Internet ads from guys in the Las Vegas area. We decided that since I was already pregnant, I no longer had to worry about letting other guys screw me, and that the "gang-bang" could include both Maria and me. Jordy sent pictures of both of us to the guys he wrote to. He got LOTS of enthusiastic replies.

We let Maria cull through "the prospects." In view of her mixed heritage, she did not care if the baby's father was white, black or Hispanic. However, she paid a lot of attention to the looks of the guys and to their claims of personal achievement, education, and personalities (to the extent that could be discerned from the letters). Jordy encouraged she select at least 10 guys, and preferably 15, since we might want to reject some at the last minute... when we met them in person.

Dutifully, Maria selected 16 guys. Jordy wrote to them and told them what weekend the three of us would be in Las Vegas. Two wrote back and told us they would not be available at that time. That still left us with 14 "possibilities".

We reserved a two-bedroom suite at one of the better hotels in Las Vegas. Maria and I were both really excited about our upcoming weekend. I think Jordy got a kick out of making all the plans for our special weekend. He gave both of us an extra good last-minute pussy trim... followed by some delightful clit licks.

We arrived early on that Friday. Jordy had already set up meetings with each of the guys, 20 minutes apart, in the lobby of our hotel. He had devised a way to recognize each of the guys. Meanwhile, Maria and I went into the hotel lounge for drinks. We sat at different locations so we wouldn't be two women together. Upon meeting each guy, Jordy brought them into the lounge to tables not too far from where we were located. That way we were both able to see the guys and observe Jordy's subtle "interviews".

We each kept notes on our observations.

As you can imagine, the "interview process" took several hours. Each time Jordy would end the interview by telling the guy he would call them later that evening and tell them where to come for the big event. When the last guy left, I had one guy that I told Jordy to drop. Maria had rejected the same guy, and one other. That left us with 12.

Jordy got on the phone and called each of the twelve guys, inviting half to join us that evening, and the other half the following evening. Then the three of us went out to dinner.

We got back to our suite about 7 PM. Maria and I showered and put on some sexy lingerie. The plan was that we would each occupy one of the bedrooms, and Jordy would do the coordination from the central living room. Maria was to not rinse her pussy between lovers, but I could. The guys were invited to arrive at different times between 8 and 9 PM.

At 7:45 there was a knock at the door. The first guy, Ted, had arrived early. Maria and I scurried to our rooms. Jordy greeted the guy as I peeked through my door. He was as handsome as his picture, and appeared to be a gentleman. Jordy let him know that he (Jordy) would be present in the living room all night, and that "you must treat both girls gently and lovingly." Then he led Ted into Maria's room. The next guy to arrive was led into my room.

My guy (Alex) kissed me and then stripped. It didn't take him long before he was eating my pussy and stroking my body. I felt so sexy and desirable as he worked his hands and lips around my body. Then he slowly entered me. I had my first orgasm moments later. After he climaxed, I thanked him and encouraged him to return to the living room so Jordy could get him into Maria's room.

As we opened the door to the living room, I found that a third guy had arrived. Jordy introduced him to me and he and I retired to my bedroom. He and I were cuddling and screwing when the door opened and Jordy told me that Bob (the fourth guy) had arrived, and that Ted and Alex were still in with Maria. Bob quickly shed his clothes and joined Alex (Mr. #3) and me on the bed. It felt great to have two previously unknown guys pressing against either side of my nude body, running their hands all over me. Jordy said, "Have fun," and stepped out of the room, closing the door behind him.

Since Mr. #3 was inside me when Bob arrived, he continued to screw me as I kissed Bob and played with his impressive cock. I felt like I was in heaven! Mr. #3 quickened his pace and soon I felt more orgasmic pleasure engulf my body, just before he shot his load into my pussy. I rolled over and began to hug and kiss him (in repayment for his gentleness with me), and Bob inserted himself into my very wet pussy.

Mr. #3 got up to clean himself up in our adjacent bathroom as Bob turned me on my tummy and began to give me some serious fucking. I know I was making a lot of noise in my enjoyment, because I heard Jordy open the door to look in and check on me. About the time I spotted him through squinty eyes that were on the verge of another orgasm, Bob started pounding me hard, and unloaded inside me.

Meanwhile, I learned later, Maria had gotten four loads of sperm pumped into her by her two first guys. One of them got dressed and went out to the living room just about the time that the last two guys arrived. As he headed out, I heard one of the new guys say to him, "You look drained." I smiled.

Jordy ushered the two new guys into Maria's room. Ted, who was Maria's first guy picked up his clothes and was asking Jordy if he could spend some time with me. Jordy brought him in, and the two guys who had been with me joined Jordy in the living room for a drink before being introduced to Maria. For a while, Maria had four guys with her. I knew she was having fun... and getting lots of the sperm she desired.

My new "lover" and I retired to my room. We made small talk, and then we took turns cleaning up in the bathroom before getting intimate. Ted was a handsome businessman... and black... my first black lover. Our session was long and leisurely, since the remaining four guys were giving all their attention to Maria... as we had planned.

Although I already had the deposits of three earlier guys coating the inside of my pussy walls, Ted got between my legs and began an oral feast that rocked me through another series of orgasms. When he finally came up for air, he crawled up beside me and played with my breasts as I used my lips and tongue to acquaint myself with his African-American skin and hair texture.

He rolled me on top of him and put his hands on my hips. He lifted my bottom up and placed my pussy right over his rigid ebony pole, letting me slide down until it was buried all the way inside me. He began rocking me back and forth, causing his cock to pull partly out, and then drive deeply into me. In spite of my recent three screwings, the feel of his cock inside me was setting me on fire again. Ted had amazing staying power! I shook my way through a few more orgasms before he flipped me over, raised my butt, and drove into me while kneeling behind me.

That time as my climax approached, I felt his cock expand within me, and then I nearly went black as his balls released their hot juices against my cervix. God I was glad that I didn't have to worry about getting pregnant.

Eventually Ted left to join Maria, and one of the last arrivals (George) slipped out of Maria's room (after having deposited his load in her), and came to my room. That time Jordy joined him. For the next hour Jordy and George played with my breasts, kissed my entire body and gave me two more screwings. As we relaxed in our afterglow, we heard Maria bid goodbye to the three guys who had still been with her. George left shortly thereafter.

I went to Maria's room for a report. I got her pillows, had her raise up, and put them under her butt. "This is just to make sure you keep all that precious sperm inside you," I told her. I cleaned up. Jordy brought us drinks. We talked for the next hour as Maria recounted her experiences, and I told her of mine.

We all cuddled, and finally fell asleep on Maria's bed.

The next night was similar to the first, except that one of the guys did not show up. We both enjoyed five guys that night (the first night Maria had six and I had five). Then, on Sunday we flew home.

As expected, within five weeks we knew Maria was pregnant. We all rejoiced. Jordy gave her one more week, just to be sure, and then gave her a celebratory screwing while I cuddled with her.

Nine months and two days after my pregnancy began, I gave birth to a healthy boy (Andrew). Roughly a month later, Maria gave birth to a tiny, but healthy girl (Beth). At age 25, Maria was a very happy mom! Maria sees herself as Andrew's aunt, and Jordy and I see ourselves uncle and aunt to Beth.

By the way, although Ted (the handsome black guy in Las Vegas) had great staying power, apparently his sperm did not win out in Maria's womb. Beth shows no signs of having a black father. She has the same lush, tan skin and black hair that her mom has. She is a beautiful baby, as is our Andrew.

Shortly after the kids were born, we decided to move to California. We now have a new, larger home in central California. Jordy was able to continue his same job with the software company. I was able to get new engineering contracts here to continue my work. Maria quit her job shortly before Beth was born, and plans to re-enter her nursing profession when Beth is a bit older.

As I write this, the kids are now two years old, and greatly enjoy playing together. Maria is now 27, I am 31 and Jordy is 32. We all still live together, and Maria has been overseeing the raising of our two kids. Life is good for all five of us!

The End

Here is a sample from another story you may enjoy:

CHOSEN TO BE

Christy's

EXTRA LOVER

HOT SEXY EROTICA

JOAN VEGAS

As I pondered what Ben was asking me about setting up a gang bang for Christy, I knew Andy and Mark would eagerly join in. But how would I discretely recruit other guys? Ben was asking me to line up at least 6 guys, in addition to me and him. I told Ben I would try. He wanted me to set it up about 5 or 6 weeks later, when he knew he would be home. And, he told me to not mention anything to Christy about our plans. He wanted to surprise her.

A few days later, I told Mark and Andy about my mission for Christy. When I told them they would be invited, they whooped and hollered. They both said they could hardly wait. I asked if they had any suggestions on how I could line up four more guys. They both suggested other guys at our school. I wasn't so sure I wanted other guys from our school knowing about the sweet deal I had with Christy and Ben.

Then Mark suggested that we put a discrete ad in one of the local alternative newspapers that was read by younger people throughout the Chicago area. After mulling over the idea, we pooled our money to place this ad for a couple of weeks: "Pretty gal wants more than one guy…soon. Write to P. O. Box ___ for details."

To our happy surprise, one of the newspapers took our ad. A week after the paper came out, the three of us got together to open the replies we had received. Wow…9 of them. Some of them included face and/or dick pictures. I was amazed. We set aside replies from older guys and married guys. We designated four of them as good prospects.

The next week, we received eleven more replies. Most of them had understood that "The pretty gal" was looking for a gang bang. They were all eager to participate. That time, we ruled out seven of them. That left us with a total of eight prospects (not counting Mark, Andy and me). I decided to contact Ben and get his opinion before we met with any of the respondents.

Again Ben and I met for a beer…alone. I told him I had two friends who were enthusiastic about the idea of helping to fulfill Christy's wish. Then I gave him the eight envelopes we had selected. He agreed that ten guys (plus he and I) might be a bit overwhelming for Christy. He set aside three of the envelopes and said, "How about if you and your friends 'interview' these other five guys." I agreed, and we finished our beers.

That evening, Ben and I had lots of fun with Christy as we winked at each other when she was turned away, knowing what we were planning for her. We made sure she got her share of orgasms that night before we each drained our nuts inside her velvety love channel.

The next day Andy, Mark and I met. I told them about Ben's decisions. We decided on a bar where we could discretely meet with the selected guys…one at a time over the next several days. They each took two guys to call, and I took one. One of Mark's contacts proved to be a flake, so we dropped him.

Over the next week, we met individually with the four remaining guys. They all seemed clean, discrete, and personable. Most importantly, they were all very eager to share in fulfilling "Mindy's" desire to be screwed by several guys. (Yes, we changed Christy's name so no one could ever come back on her.) We got their contact phone numbers, told them the tentative time, and told them we would be calling with a hotel location where we would be meeting.

Ben arranged for a hotel suite and told Christy to be ready for an extra special evening with me and him giving her lots of passionate loving. She bought it.

Shortly after Ben and Christy arrived in the hotel room, I came in (I had my own key card). He and I necked with her while stripping off her clothes. We got her onto the middle of the large bed and Ben began to eat her. I told them I had to go get some ice for our drinks, and left Christy to enjoy Ben's oral ministrations.

I ran downstairs and met Mark and Andy. I brought them to the suite and had them quietly remove their clothes as I made noise mixing drinks for Christy and Ben. In the background, Andy and Mark were both stroking themselves to hardness. I walked into the bedroom with a drink in each hand saying, "You guys ready for some liquid refreshment?" They both sat up and reached for a drink.

Then I looked at Christy and asked, "Are you ready for some extra pleasure?" That was my cue to Mark and Andy. They walked in behind me, totally naked, with boners sticking out in front of them. I said, "Christy…this is Mark and this Andy…my friends…here to give you some extra pleasure." Christy grinned at my nude friends. Ben had already stood up. He said, "Christy baby, I hope you enjoy this special evening," and he sat in a nearby chair.

Andy dove between Christy's outstretched legs and began to lick on her pussy. Although I was still dressed, I got on the bed, cuddled Christy into my arms, and gave her a big kiss. Meanwhile, Mark laid on the bed on the other side of Christy and began caressing her body. He took one of her hands and wrapped it around his stiff dick.

Christy whispered into my ear, "What's going on?" I told her, "Tonight you are going to get your vagina eaten and screwed to your heart's content. Enjoy yourself." She grinned at me before rolling to face Mark. "You are Mark, huh?" she said, while squeezing his dick. "My," she said, "your dick is very hard. I'll bet you know how to use it." She threw her arm over his shoulder and gave him a hot kiss.

If you enjoyed this sample, look for **Chosen to be Christy's Extra Lover.**

Here is another sample you may also like:

A
THREE-WAY
ROMP

Katherine's Birthday Surprise

Three-Way Romps, Book I
CARLY DEANE

As she came through the door her radiant green eyes instantly flamed in shock and very appreciative surprise at the sight of Darius' unabashed look of animal hunger that he didn't even bother to conceal. I didn't and couldn't blame him and once again I thanked the Sex Gods for the day I'd met my perfect sexual soul mate in Katherine Webster…because there she was and it was glorious!

Her long, luxurious mane of rich scarlet hair flowed past her slender shoulders framing her exquisitely fine ivory features that some might've said were perhaps almost too delicate were it not for the ripe, lush strawberry lips. I knew she knew exactly how to use them and loved doing it. Her deep emerald eyes were already inflamed by the sight of Darius' combination of cultured manliness and brutally evident vigor.

She was wearing a light jade colored blouse that was sheer on top and displayed to perfect advantage the eruption of her creamy bosoms molded to a black sheer bra that just barely peeked out from the blouse to wink at our drooling mouths.

Her white, just above-the-knees length silk skirt might have possibly fit in at her law office, if she hadn't finished it with the sultry addition of sheer black, thigh-high hose hooked to garters and with a sexy seam running up the back. I knew they were thigh-highs and now Darius did too because she stopped and did her "flamingo" leg show for us both, grabbing one black stiletto off with her hand as her skirt rose up against the rising tide of her tight thighs.

She stood there with her best *little-girl-lost* look and at 28 she could really sell it. We could also see that the scarlet pedicure on her dainty toes matched her flaming hair deliciously. She was definitely flaming on both ends and I was sure we were all about to turn up the heat in the middle.

"Oooooh….sorry…do I have to remove my heels here Darren honey?"

But she burned Darius with a look when she said it.

"Birthday girl, you can take off whatever you want here."

She bent over at the waist and gave us a shot of her luscious, heart-shaped ass that was stretching that white skirt to its limit. Then she slipped off the other stiletto and flipped her fall of crimson silk around her lovely face. She glanced provocatively back with a distinct hint of naughty girl in her green eyes that told the two of us in a deliciously unspoken but perfectly clear way that she was definitely down for the night's action. And it was time for *action!*

"Darren! He's always such a bad boy....don't you think so Mister Friend?" She said in mock shock as she levelled Darius with her sparkling greens. So the Game was ON!

I spoke up quickly to get the gears in motion.

"Oh, sorry baby...this is my old friend Darius". I looked at him and he looked like he wanted to tackle her right there. "...I don't think you've ever met him although of course I've mentioned you before...Darius, this is my main lady, Katherine."

"Pleased to meet you at last Katherine," he nailed her with a look that said he wanted to score and she matched his naked enthusiasm with equal passion, "did somebody say that this is your birthday?"

We both stood up as Darius rose to give her a full display of all 6'3" of him and I grinned hard with anticipation as she eagerly drank in every inch with a sly smile. Her blazing eyes lingered just a second too long to be considered decent on his bulging crotch that was threatening to launch her excitement without any countdown.

The fine cream of her skin flushed visibly but she managed to toss her heels aside nonchalantly and strode slowly but very confidently into the room treating us both to the wondrous waves of bouncing tits and her undulating hips that promised power and pleasure all around.

"It is but please don't ask me which one because a lady never tells..."

In three and a half years of us playing this game, I'd never seen Kathy so instantly turned on before. I could almost smell her juices flowing as she sauntered up to Darius and extended her hand while ever so slightly sliding her tongue along her juicy lips.

This alone told me that she had started her own celebration a little early, probably with at least a few glasses of wine to get her engine lubed. When their fingers touched it was like sexual lightning had just struck the room and I was feeling the energy surging straight into my cock that was already bouncing up and down like a happy dog's tail.

"Well Darren...where do you think I should sit?"

She asked coquettishly finally releasing Darius' fingers while tilting her shoulders forward just enough to present her gorgeous display of beautiful, all-natural "C"s to our mutual delight. Those lush tits that tasted like sweet wine didn't fall out of that silky bra but it was a close call. Darius threw her a dazzling winner of a smile and I just knew that we could get right to it with as little of the niceties as necessary.

"Why don't you place that beautiful derriere of yours right in the middle of us baby?"

I indicated the well space in the tatami and she immediately sashayed around the table, up to me and buried her tits in my chest, giving me a full blast of her feminine heat as she planted a tasty peck of her steamy lips on mine while not-so-subtly brushing my cock with her hand.

"MMMmmm…that sounds like a great idea baby but…do you think we'll all fit?"

She winked at me then stroked me again giving my rod a nice boost. It was her signal of approval and I was starving to get at her.

I could see that Darius had not missed the cock stroke and I could also see that he was getting the idea quickly as I shot him a wink too just as Kathy slipped her legs under the table and sat down with her face looking up at Darius' crotch. I sat beside her and noticed that Darius was not making any special effort to hide his own excitement as what looked like a thick cable of muscle formed in his tight pants and he made no move to sit down.

"Maybe I can get a kiss from the birthday girl too…" he winked back and continued, "…what do you say Darren…can a brother get a break?"

"Oh I think Katherine definitely has a lot of love to give on this very special occasion…" I hit them both with a knowing look, "…and I trust Darius all the way baby."

"Trust" was our three-way code word and I could see the immediate thrill in her sparkling greens when she heard it.

Then I took her hand and held her as she stood up facing Darius and, after slowly readjusting her skirt, leaned into him, lifted herself up on her toes and kissed him full on the mouth, teasing her tongue on his lips as she brushed her hand boldly against his swelling cock meat.

The sight of her kissing and stroking this modern day Mandingo with sultry abandon made my own cock jump up and suddenly I couldn't stand up again even if I'd wanted to.

"Oh…My Goodness!"

Kathy purred as she barely broke free from their kiss that had rocked me to my bone. She was fully flushed and quaking after having felt the evident and enormous virility of what was in store for her.

I couldn't wait a moment longer and so as she stared into Darius' now fiery brown eyes that were burning with lust I grabbed her bulging ass cheeks with both hands. Then I lifted her skirt just enough to smell the heavy scent of her juicy excitement as I leaned my face into the ambrosia of her ass.

"DARREN!"

She mock protested but I detected a very real quiver in her voice.

Often just as we dove into our threes I'd noticed that unmistakable quiver that meant she was turned on in a very real, very physical sense. This unmistakable sign of her body's surrender to passion was absolutely her one and only kryptonite.

Having heard it I suddenly didn't care if Darius joined in our game or not because I wanted a deep dip into the honey of her sweet pussy. I wanted to lap up that flowing sauce until she fully surrendered, moaned and begged me, or *us*, to fuck the hell out of her.

"What will Darius think…?"

She almost whispered but then kissed him quickly again before he could reply or say anything to buckle the momentum.

"Darius can think what he wants and he can do what he wants baby…but I need some of this juicy pussy, birthday girl…and I need it now!"

I slid my hands along her hips to the side zipper of her tight skirt then pulled it down and smoothly slipped it past her hips and off and she eagerly squirmed to make the journey even shorter. The nectar of her pussy flooded my nostrils as I tossed her skirt aside and the full moon of her gorgeous ass glowed in my hungry face.

There were no panties in the way so I snapped one of her garters and I heard her gasp of- *Hhuunnnhh-* although her lips did not break from Darius' and she made no move to stop me. Her tongue was sunk into Darius' mouth and he had his own eyes closed and was obviously and enthusiastically responding in full.

So I grabbed her now bare hips and pulled her steamy pussy into my mouth as I looked up and saw her vigorously and wondrously stroking Darius' meat openly and without any pretension. I forcefully grabbed the tight cheeks of her ample ass and spread them gently, just the way I knew she liked it, and dove in. She was drenched and my mouth was immediately covered in her steamy pussy juice as I licked and sucked up all I could get, teasing her clit with my tongue just to make her lose control.

"Mmmm…good pussy…mmmmm…yea!"

I grabbed her hips and jammed my face deeper into her ass with my drenched lips completely covering her burning labia, my tongue applied directly to her clit and my nose buried in the taboo fragrance of her near virgin asshole. I slobbered and slurped at her steamy slit in complete abandon, to hell with technique. From the corner of my eyes I could see her and Darius still sucking away at each other's tongues even as she groaned her pussy pleasure.

"MMMMmmmmmmmmmmmmmmm…"

As I lapped away greedily, I sensed that the moans had pushed whatever reserve Darius may have felt over the edge and he gave in as well. I could see his massive hands groping wildly at her breasts as she reached down and passionately fondled his ass. She urged him on even more as he skillfully worked the buttons on her blouse as they finally broke their kiss and she shrugged off her silky top, offering her heaving breasts to his lips.

"Suck me Darius, please suck me…I want it…I love it!"

He didn't need any instruction as he dove ravenously on her rosebud nipples doing some aggressive slurping of his own even as I lapped up the flood of juices that poured from her inflamed pussy. The surging river of her sex juices told me all I needed to know about her state of near explosion and as I saw her grabbing at Darius' cock greedily I knew she was ready for anything. Her quavering words said the rest.

"Take it out Darius…give it to me…please…"

And then Darius, drunk from the booze and even drunker from her flesh, proved that he was more than a match for the game and that he had some moves left in him as he tore himself from her breasts, ripped off his own shirt and then unbuckled his pants as I lapped away at the fountain of her flowing pussy.

"Alright, birthday girl…you ready to suck some big, black cock…whatchu think Darren…this beautiful little white girl ready for some Brooklyn black snake?"

His voice was teasing but hard and I didn't need to reply because she took care of that herself as she feverishly pulled at his pants then reached in to free his giant dick for her pleasure.

"Yes, I'm ready… give it to me Darius… Oh… ooohhh… my… god!"

If you enjoy this sample, look for <u>**A Three-Way Romp: Three-Way Romps, Book 1 by Carly Deane**</u>.

Also by this Author:

Nine Guys Share Their Wives

Sharing Husbands

A Game for Three

18 Guys on Being the Extra Guy

Aussie Wife gets Naughty

Wife Enjoys Pleasure of MFM

Our Studly Neighbor

A Taste of MFM

The Stinging Nettle

Wife Sharing Fiesta

Caught in the Midst of Two

Sandwiched by Two

The More, The Merrier

Fooled - Pleasured - Pleased

Love Can Handle It

Scottish Affair

White Wives, Black Lovers

Swinger's Dilemma

Share the Love

When In Spain

From the Author

If you enjoyed this book, check out the several other works by Joan Vegas at http://www.amazon.co.uk/Joan-Vegas/e/B00A49TPAS.

Check my page on Amazon and my blog for Updates and interesting info.

Author Central Page - http://amzn.to/14ZEmfs
Author Blog - http://joan-vegas.awesomeauthors.org/

If you enjoyed any of my books then please share the love and click like on my books in Amazon.

If you write me a review and send me an email I will send you a free book, or many.
(Just know that these emails are filtered by my publisher.)

Good news is always welcome.

One Last Thing, For Kindle Readers...

When you turn the page, Kindle will give you the opportunity to rate this book and share your thoughts on Facebook and Twitter. If you enjoyed my writings, would you please take a few seconds to let your friends know about it? Because... when they enjoy they will be grateful to you and so will I.

Thank You!

Joan Vegas
joan_vegas@awesomeauthors.org

About the Author

Joan Vegas was born in 1973 and grew up in a small town in mid-USA.

After graduating from college, she met two guys. Both were really special and she fell in love with both of them. She was fortunate that they love her so much. They then decided to "share" her. The three of them moved in together, later on forming a "family partnership". They eventually had four children together (the story behind it is very interesting).

Because of their unique three-way partnership family, she has gotten to know other couples where a third person was regularly a part of their intimate relationships. It is the correspondence to/from these other advocates of three-way intimacy relationships that Joan's true reports are based on. And yes, it can happen... It can be very fun, intimate, and wonderful!

"Thank you for reading my stories/reports. If you are part of a three-way intimate relationship, I would love to hear from you."

www.ingramcontent.com/pod-product-compliance
Lightning Source LLC
Chambersburg PA
CBHW071353130626
46556CB00005B/2167